PAW PATROL™: PUPS SAVE THE FLYING FOOD
A CENTUM BOOK 9781912707386
Published in Great Britain by Centum Books Ltd
This edition published 2018
1 3 5 7 9 10 8 6 4 2

Centum Books Ltd, 20 Devon Square, Newton Abbot, Devon TQ12 2HR, UK
books@centumbooksltd.co.uk
CENTUM BOOKS Limited Reg. No. 07641486

A CIP catalogue record for this book is
available from the British Library

Printed in Poland

PUPS SAVE THE FLYING FOOD

STARRING . . .

ROCKY

RUBBLE

MARSHALL

SKYE

CHASE

RYDER

Mr Porter has found a great new way to deliver food around Adventure Bay.

"My drones can deliver really quickly," he tells Ryder. "One of them is on the way to the Lookout right now with a bag full of yummy treats!"

In just a few seconds the drone arrives at the Lookout. It's just behind a worried-looking Marshall.

"Help! A bug is chasing me," he cries.

"Don't worry. It's not a bad bug. It's carrying tasty treats for us," laughs Ryder.

The drones are doing a great job around Adventure Bay. Mayor Goodway is delighted when one of them brings her a delicious bayberry cream pie. Captain Turbot is thrilled to get his favourite squid ice cream. There's even some extra squid for Wally!

Everybody loves
the super-quick drone
service and Mr Porter is
getting busier and busier.
It's all going smoothly
until ... *SPLAT*. He drops
his drone remote control
in a bayberry pie!

"Come back," he cries
as a drone picks up the
pie and flies off into
the distance.

The drone flies over Yumi's Farm and drops the pie straight into the pig pen ... *SPLOSH!*

When the piglets find the remote control they start pressing the buttons....

Suddenly, every drone in town starts dropping food. Pizza, vegetables and ice cream splat down onto the streets below. Even Alex's paddling pool fills up with pies – with Alex still sitting in it!

"There's only one thing I can do ... call the PAW Patrol," says Mr Porter.

Ryder takes the call as pizza splats onto the Lookout windows outside.

"Don't worry," he tells Mr Porter. "No job is too messy, no pup is too small. PAW Patrol to the Air Patroller!"

The pups are soon on board the Air Patroller, ready for action.

"Thanks pups. Drones are dropping food everywhere and we've got to stop them," Ryder explains.

"Sounds like a messy mission, but a yummy one, too," says Rubble.

"You'll need your flight packs for this one," Ryder tells the pups. "Rocky, use your claw to catch food before it lands on people.

Rubble, use your hoverboard to swat away flying food.

Marshall, you'll need your water cannons to clean any mess we miss."

PAW Patrol is on a roll!

The three pups are soon airborne, heading for the drones. Rocky dives into action and uses his claw arm to grab an ice-cream sundae just before it lands on Mayor Goodway.

"My hero!" she says.

Marshall uses his water cannons to clean sticky pizza off the street while Rubble swats away flying food.

He saves some of his favourite carrots to munch on and drops a spare carrot down to one of his rabbit friends below.

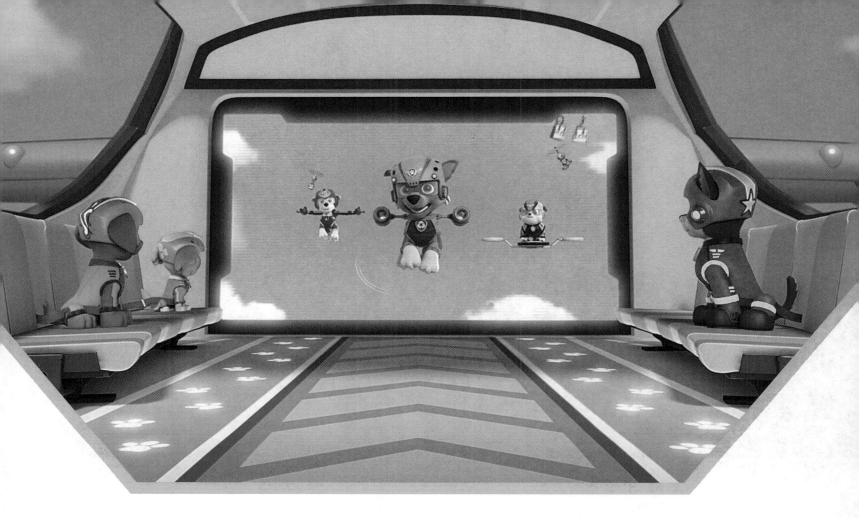

"Great flying, pups," says Ryder over the PupPad video screen.
"Thanks, but there are just too many drones and too much food
for us to handle," Rocky replies as food keeps raining down.
"Don't worry. I have an idea," says Ryder.

"Chase, we need you to catch a drone in your safety net. Rocky, you can reprogramme it with your screwdriver to activate its homing device," explains Ryder. "The homing device will fly the drone back to the remote control."

"Chase is on the case!"

Chase says and zooms out to join the messy mission.

"Ruff! Safety net," orders Chase and his net shoots out to trap a drone.

"Nice catch, Chase," cries Rocky. "Ruff, ruff. Screwdriver!" His screwdriver appears and he uses it to reprogramme the drone before letting it go.

"Now it's your turn, Skye," says Ryder.

"Gotta fly!" says Skye and soon she is on the drone's tail. It's a wild ride around the rooftops of Adventure Bay, but she never lets the drone out of her sights.

At last the drone hovers over the pig pen at Yumi's Farm.

"Oh no! It's picked up two piglets," cries Skye, "and the remote control is here but it's not working properly. I think the piglets have been playing with it."

Suddenly, the remote control buzzes and flashes, and all the drones in town switch off at once. Even more food splats down and so do a few drones.

One of them crash -lands in a field and one ends up like a hat on the Mayor's Chickaletta statue.

The piglets are dropped, too. They're on a crash course for Mr Porter's restaurant! Just in time Ryder sees the paddling pool full of pie.

"That will make the perfect piggy landing pad," he says.

"Chase, can you get down there? I'm coming, too." Ryder zooms out of the Air Patroller ready for action.

Chase uses his turbo jets to help him push the pool into position.
"Forward ... a bit more ... stop right there," directs Ryder.

SPLOSH!

The piglets
land safely in
the soft pie mix.

"Thanks PAW Patrol," says Mr Porter. "I think I might give up on drones and go back to my trusty delivery van from now on."

"That sounds like a good idea. And remember: if you're ever in trouble again, just yelp for help," says Ryder.

"There's just one more thing to do ..."

"Someone's got to rescue those little piglets from that delicious pie mix. That'll be me," says Rubble and he dives in with a shout.

Yummiest rescue ever!

THE END